Bear-ly There

Rebekah Raye

Bears for You
for
Anthony Olivia
and Michael

With love
Rebekah Raye
2012

Tilbury House, Publishers
Gardiner, Maine

Spring finally arrived.
Warm sun reached through the spruce
branches, melting patches of crusty snow on the hillside.
Whisps of steam rose from a pile of rocks near
a fallen tree. Suddenly a bear poked
his head out of his winter den.

It was a black bear, waking up after a six-month nap through the cold winter months. The bear stretched and pulled himself out of the den, shaking off dirt and leaves. He stood up on his tall hind legs to view and smell the area. (His nose could smell things far, far away.) The bear was very hungry, but first he leaned against the base of a pine tree, rubbing his soft, furry back up and down, back and forth, against the rough bark. It felt wonderful, and this also left his scent to tell other bears he was there.

The bear noticed cutworms rising and squirming through the moist dirt at his feet. He lay down on his belly to lick them up. His big claws dug deeper to find a few buried acorns and some tasty plant roots. He continued to forage for food, making his way through the woods as the stars came out in the evening sky.

Then something in the air—a sweet, nutty odor—led him down the hill and out of the woods. Beyond the meadow that bordered the woods, there were houses. That delicious smell came from a shed next to one of the houses.

Charlie lived in that house with his parents. Behind the house were two small sheds. A chickenwire fence made a yard for Charlie's two pet geese. In the daytime they grazed on the first new blades of green grass and swam in their pool. At night they slept in one of the sheds, where they had their nests. Charlie stacked bales of straw for their bedding in the other shed, which also held metal garbage cans full of grain for the geese and sunflower seeds for the bird feeders.

Every evening just before dark, Charlie made sure the geese were safe in their shed for the night. When the geese were young goslings, he made up a song to lead them to bed. With his hands slapping the sides of his legs in rhythm, he sang,

Hop, hop, hop

Time to go to bed

Hop, hop, hop

Time to go to bed

Hop, hop, hop

Time to go to bed

Time to go to bed,

my gooossseyyysss.

He liked the end, when he hissed like a goose! Now, when they heard the song, the two smart geese marched right up the ramp into their shed and settled down for the night.

Charlie wanted
to keep his geese
safe from other
creatures who
might wander around
the backyard after dark.
On some nights raccoons squeezed underneath
the fence looking for leftover grain. Charlie even saw one
go for a swim in the goose pool! Sometimes a family of skunks searched for
insects or leftovers in the compost pile. He spotted a bobcat one night and
a fox another night, each looking for mice who were interested in the
leftover grain and seeds. With all those visitors, Charlie only slept soundly
when he knew the geese were safe in their shed.

Later that night Charlie woke to a terrifying loud cracking noise! His heart pounded as he bolted out of bed. He crept to the window and in the moonlight saw a tall black shape at the storage shed. It was a bear! Charlie's first worry was for his geese, but they were being very, very quiet in the other shed. As Charlie watched, the bear ripped at the shed door with his sharp claws, pushing and pulling until it broke in half—and the way was clear.

The bear pulled the can of sunflower seeds toward him, tilting it on its side. Seeds scattered everywhere, and the bear lay down on his belly and started to lick them up.

Charlie's parents hurried down the hall to his room, turning on the light as they burst in. They joined Charlie at the window, staring at the bear in disbelief.

When the bear saw them all in the sudden light, he lumbered off quickly.

"What if the bear comes back?" Charlie asked. "I don't want him to eat the geese!"

"I think he is interested in the birdseed, not the geese," his dad said. "I'll repair the shed door in the morning. We'll move the birdseed and grain into the cellar, where the bear can't smell them."

After breakfast, Charlie went outside
and found some of the bear's paw prints.
He put his hand near one and saw how
much bigger the bear's paw was. The bear
had been almost as tall as the shed. And he
must have been super strong to break the
door in two.

Later that day, Charlie walked down the lane to get the mail at the
post office. Mrs. Kelly was pulling weeds along her fence. Charlie told her
about the bear. She wondered if it might have been the same bear that
pulled her bird feeder off its post and ate all the seeds. She said a neighbor
told her a bear had torn apart his compost pile. He wanted to call the game
warden to have the bear trapped and relocated. Another neighbor was
worried that the bear might hurt his sheep and goats. He talked about
shooting the bear.

Walking home, Charlie turned into the lane just as the neighbor's cat, Black Velvet, streaked by. Then he heard loud honking, and suddenly his two geese flew right over the fence and coasted onto the neighbor's lawn.

Charlie slowly looked around the corner of the house—there was the bear! When he saw Charlie, he turned and ran up the hill. The bird feeder was on the ground, empty. The compost pile was torn up and scattered over the lawn. It was time to come up with a plan to keep the bear where he belonged—in the woods.

That evening,
after Charlie finished his
homework and was about to
put the geese to bed, he looked out
the window. He saw the bear coming down the hill.
Charlie ran to get his mom and dad and they each picked up
the items they would need. They waited quietly outside, around the corner
of the house, until the bear reached the storage shed—then they did it!

CLANG! BANG! CLANG!

Charlie clashed the cymbals from his drum set.

BANG! BANG! BANG!

Mom bashed some pot lids.

But his dad made
the most noise of all.
He squeezed the trigger
on the air horn from
their boat. It made a
HUGE honk
that blasted through the night!
The geese added their honks. The sparrows
and blue jays and mourning doves all flew
from the trees. That great big bear tucked
his small tail between his legs and ran for the
hill as fast as he could. Dad let out another
blast of the horn as the bear disappeared into
the woods. That was almost the last
they saw of the bear.

One afternoon in late summer Charlie and his parents went for a picnic in the nearby hills where the wild blueberries were ready for picking. Charlie loved blueberry pies, blueberry jam, and blueberry muffins, so he made sure he filled his berry boxes to the very top.

They weren't the only ones enjoying the berries. Charlie heard a group of crows cawing loudly at the other side of the meadow.

He looked toward the crows. Without saying a word, he quietly tapped his parents on their arms and pointed.

*J*ust below them, in a thick blueberry patch,
a fat, shiny black bear was looking back at them.
The bear stood up to sniff the air. Sensing possible
danger, he quickly ran into the shadows of the forest.

Charlie smiled. "Look—you can barely see him.
He was finding his dinner where he should.
That's sure better than seeing him in our backyard!"

TILBURY HOUSE, PUBLISHERS

103 Brunswick Avenue

Gardiner, ME 04345

800-582-1899

www.tilburyhouse.com

First hardcover edition: October 2009 • 10 9 8 7 6 5 4 3 2 1

For Ahlyisen

And with thanks to the special "Charlies" in my life

And to Mama Goose and Goosey Goose

Library of Congress Cataloging-in-Publication Data

Raye, Rebekah.

Bear-ly there / Rebekah Raye. — 1st hardcover ed.

p. cm.

Summary: When a big black bear shows up at Charlie's house one moonlit night and breaks into a shed to eat the grain that is stored there, Charlie and his parents devise a plan to make sure the bear stays in the woods where it belongs.

ISBN 978-0-88448-314-4 (hardcover : alk. paper)

[1. Bears—Fiction. 2. Country life—Fiction.] I. Title. II. Title: Bearly there.

PZ7.R21036Be 2009

[E]—dc22

2009027314

Designed by Geraldine Millham, Westport, Massachusetts.

Printed by Sung In Printing, Gyeonggi, South Korea, August 2009.